Dear Parents:

Congratulations! Your child is taking
the first steps on an exciting journey.
The destination? Independent reading!

STEP INTO READING® will help your child get there. The program offers
five steps to reading success. Each step includes fun stories and colorful
art or photographs. In addition to original fiction and books with favorite
characters, there are Step into Reading Non-Fiction Readers, Phonics Readers
and Boxed Sets, Sticker Readers, and Comic Readers—a complete literacy
program with something to interest every child.

Learning to Read, Step by Step!

Ready to Read   Preschool–Kindergarten
• big type and easy words • rhyme and rhythm • picture clues
For children who know the alphabet and are eager to
begin reading.

Reading with Help   Preschool–Grade 1
• basic vocabulary • short sentences • simple stories
For children who recognize familiar words and sound out
new words with help.

Reading on Your Own   Grades 1–3
• engaging characters • easy-to-follow plots • popular topics
For children who are ready to read on their own.

Reading Paragraphs   Grades 2–3
• challenging vocabulary • short paragraphs • exciting stories
For newly independent readers who read simple sentences
with confidence.

Ready for Chapters   Grades 2–4
• chapters • longer paragraphs • full-color art
For children who want to take the plunge into chapter books
but still like colorful pictures.

STEP INTO READING® is designed to give every child a successful
reading experience. The grade levels are only guides; children will progress
through the steps at their own speed, developing confidence in their reading.

Remember, a lifetime love of reading starts with a single step!

Step into Reading, Random House, and the Random House colophon are registered trademarks of Penguin Random House LLC.

Visit us on the Web!
StepIntoReading.com
randomhousekids.com

Educators and librarians, for a variety of teaching tools, visit us at RHTeachersLibrarians.com

ISBN 978-0-7364-3809-4 (trade) — ISBN 978-0-7364-8252-3 (lib. bdg.)
ISBN 978-0-7364-3810-0 (ebook)

Printed in the United States of America 10 9 8 7 6 5 4 3 2 1

DISNEP · PIXAR

COCO

A Family Mystery

adapted by Sarah Hernandez

illustrated by the Disney Storybook Art Team

Random House 🏠 New York

Miguel Rivera lives in Mexico
with his big family.

Mamá Coco is
his great-grandmother.
Miguel loves her.

Before Miguel was born,
the Rivera home
was filled with music.
One day, Coco's papá left
to play music
all over the world.
He never came back.

Coco's mother is Mamá Imelda.
Imelda learned to make shoes
to help her family.
She has one rule:
NO MUSIC!

Miguel's abuelita

has the same rule.

But Miguel has a secret.

He does not want

to make shoes

like his family.

He loves music!

He sings and plays guitar

for his dog, Dante.

Ernesto de la Cruz is
Miguel's favorite musician.
Miguel knows all
his songs and movies.
He wants to be
just like Ernesto.

Miguel wants to play
in a talent show
on Día de los Muertos,
the Day of the Dead.
That is when family
in the Land of the Dead
visit the Land of the Living.

For Día de los Muertos,
the Riveras put photos
of their family
on an altar.

In a photo of Mamá Coco
when she was little,
her papá has a guitar.
It is Ernesto's!
Mamá Coco's papá is
Ernesto de la Cruz!

Abuelita says Miguel cannot
play in the talent show.
The family rule
is no music!

She smashes his guitar.

Miguel runs away.

He needs a new instrument.

He finds Ernesto's guitar
and plays it.

Suddenly,
Miguel can see
his family from
the Land of the Dead!
They are skeletons.

His family will take him
to Mamá Imelda.
Miguel needs a blessing
from a family member.
Then he can return
to the Land of the Living.

But Imelda's blessing
comes with
a condition:
no music.
Miguel runs off.

He meets Hector.

Hector knows Ernesto de la Cruz!

Miguel tells him Ernesto

is his only family member

and Miguel needs his blessing.

Hector will help Miguel

find Ernesto.

In return, Miguel will bring
Hector's photo to the
Land of the Living.
Hector paints Miguel
to look like a skeleton
so he will fit in.

Miguel enters a talent show.

Hector plays onstage with him.

The talent show host

says there is a family

looking for a live boy.

But Hector thought Ernesto
was Miguel's only family!
Miguel lied to him.
Miguel thinks Hector
will not help him find Ernesto.
He throws
Hector's photo at him.

Mamá Imelda finds Miguel.

She says he must choose

between family and music.

Miguel does not want to choose.

He storms off.

Miguel finds Ernesto
at his mansion.
Miguel plays a song.
Ernesto is happy to meet his
great-great-grandson!

Hector appears.

He and Ernesto used

to be friends.

But Hector is not happy

to see Ernesto.

Miguel finds out that Ernesto
stole Hector's songs
and his guitar!
Ernesto does not want
anyone to know.
He throws Hector and Miguel
into a pit!

If they are not rescued by sunrise,
Miguel will turn into a skeleton!

Hector used to write songs
for his daughter, Coco.
Mamá Coco is Hector's daughter!
Hector is Miguel's
great-great-grandfather!
If Coco does not remember Hector,
he will disappear.

Mamá Imelda saves
Hector and Miguel.
Everyone learns the truth
about Ernesto.

Hector and Imelda give Miguel
their blessing to go home.

Miguel sings Hector's song
to Mamá Coco.

The whole family watches.

She remembers Papá Hector!

Music fills their home
once again.

The Rivera family
love each other,
and they love music, too.
Music brings them
all together.